"Any book without a mistake in it has had too much money spent on it"

Sir William Collins, publisher

Vampires

NIGEL SUCKLING

ff&f

Vampires

Published by
Facts, Figures & Fun, an imprint of
AAPPL Artists' and Photographers' Press Ltd.
10 Hillside, London SW19 4NH, UK
info@ffnf.co.uk www.ffnf.co.uk
info@aappl.com www.aappl.com

Sales and Distribution
UK and export: Turnaround Publisher Services Ltd.
orders@turnaround-uk.com
USA and Canada: Sterling Publishing Inc.
sales@sterlingpub.com
Australia & New Zealand: Peribo Pty.
peribomec@bigpond.com
South Africa: Trinity Books. trinity@iafrica.com

A catalogue record for this book is available
from the British Library.

ISBN 13: 9781904332480
ISBN 10: 190433248X

Design (contents and cover): Malcolm Couch
mal.couch@blueyonder.co.uk

Printed in China by Imago Publishing
info@imago.co.uk

Contents

Introduction

IN ONE FORM OR ANOTHER, vampires have haunted the dreams and nightmares of every known culture, but the vampire most people think of today originates mainly from Eastern Europe.

Christopher Lee, arguably the most suave and sophisticated screen vampire ever, once suggested that Dracula's appeal lies in his being a wish-fulfilment figure for both sexes. For men he offers the model of a superman with absolute power over the women he desires, untrammelled by civilised notions of fairness, consideration or fidelity. For women, said Lee, he appeals to their secret desire to surrender to such absolute mastery, to sublimate their own will and identity in that of a dominant male. Brave words!

The word 'vampire' is probably of Slavonic origin, as in the Magyar *wampir*. Slight variations of the word occur in most tongues of the Balkans and Eastern Europe, though in Greece vampires are more commonly called *vrykolakas*, a term they share with werewolves, to whom they are closely related and which means something like 'wolf-fairy'.

Historically and in fiction, vampires are the undead. Or, strictly speaking, they are the dead who steal an unnatural extension of their earthly existence by rising physically from the grave and drinking the lifeblood of others. They are not technically demons, which are spiritual beings that can occasionally take on the semblance of physical form, though they can be demonic enough in their behaviour. Vampires have supernatural powers of shape-shifting and within certain limits can come and go as they please within the hours of darkness.

The first victims of a vampire are usually their family and friends.

Throughout Christendom it was once held that murderers and suicides were likely to rise again as hungry ghosts or vampires, for which reason they were buried at crossroads to minimise the chance of them finding their way home. Often as added precautions a wooden stake was driven through their hearts and/or their heads were cut off.

In Britain a law requiring suicides to be buried at cross-roads with a stake through the heart was only repealed around 1824.

In Western Christianity it was mainly the ghosts of the unhappy dead that people feared, but in the East it was believed they could take a much more physical form – that of vampires as we think of them today.

COMMON CAUSES OF
BECOMING A VAMPIRE

Inheriting the condition from a parent

Being bitten by a vampire (if you survive)

Drinking the blood of a vampire

Having your corpse exposed to the
light of the full moon
(especially if you have been murdered)

Committing suicide or suffering a violent death

Being a sorcerer or werewolf in life

WAYS TO RECOGNISE
A VAMPIRE

Aversion to sunlight

Pale skin, red eyes and foul breath

Lack of reflection in a mirror

Hairy palms of the hand

Bushy eyebrows which join over the nose

In Bulgaria vampires have only one nostril

In Poland they have a sharp point like a bee's
sting on the tip of their tongues

Small finger-sized holes around the edge of
its grave

Lack of decomposition in the grave
(unless the person happens to be a saint)

WAYS TO DEFEND AGAINST
A VAMPIRE

Wear strings of garlic and have it draped
around windows and doors

Holy water, crucifixes, rosaries and any other
(not necessarily Christian) sacred symbols, though
these appear (in fiction at least) to have diminishing
power these days. Possibly the wielder of such
symbols has to believe in their holiness

Nailing the corpse of potential vampires to the
base of their coffins with iron nails, preferably
through the skull

Stuffing garlic into the mouth of a potential vampire
and spreading garlic, thorns and poppy seeds in and
around the coffin

In Bulgaria it was once a common practice for
vampire hunters to *bottle* them. They would chase
the vampires with a fragment of some holy icon
and corner them till they had no choice but to
hide in a bottle containing some human blood,
then it was sealed with a cork to which the icon
was fixed. The bottle would be buried in some
out-of-the-way place in the hope that no-one
would disturb it

WAYS TO DESTROY
A VAMPIRE

Drive a wooden stake with a single blow through
the heart. The stake should preferably be aspen,
maple, hawthorn or whitethorn

If you strike a second blow the vampire
will revive

Behead the vampire and ensure that the head
cannot get back by stuffing the neck with garlic or
salt, and wedging the head between the knees

Remove the heart and burn it to ashes

Burn the whole vampire to ashes and scatter them

All of the above

In the Eastern Orthodox Church it was once dogma that the bodies of excommunicates did not decompose in the usual way because their spirits were still attached. For which reason they were likely to rise again as vampires unless precautions were taken.

The fifteenth century Sultan of Turkey, Mohammed II, arch-enemy of the original Dracula, was intrigued by the supposed power of excommunication to prevent post-mortem decay amongst his Christian subjects. Summoning the Orthodox Patriarch of Istanbul, Maximus, the Sultan demanded a demonstration.

A search was made for the grave of a woman famously excommunicated for promiscuity. The body was exhumed and (no doubt to Maximus' great relief) found to be in the predicted condition – dark-skinned and swollen as a drum, but with no other sign of decomposition.

Then came the real test. The coffin was carried to the palace and sealed under the Sultan's gaze. Then it was taken to church and a service of abso- lution performed over it by the Patriarch, witnessed by a number of trusted courtiers (though not the Sultan himself, who presumably did not wish to compromise his Islamic faith).

The story goes that halfway through the service there came a rattle of bones from the coffin, and when it was opened the body was found to have been reduced to dust.

In Greece until recently wizards, witches and anyone dying with unconfessed mortal sins on their consciences were also believed likely to become vampires; plus anyone dying with a curse on their heads (even their own, which must have made people think twice before saying "damn me"!), or any corpse over which a cat or wild animal had jumped – which was one reason for keeping vigil over the dead before they were safely buried.

So great was the fear of becoming a vampire from curses either directed at, or received from others that a ritual was devised to prevent it. Dying people in Greece traditionally gathered their friends, family and, if possible, their enemies around them and dissolved some salt in water, saying 'as this salt dissolves, so my curses dissolve'. Everyone else then took back all the curses they had directed towards the dying person.

Murder victims in Greece were once believed also likely to become vampires if their death was not avenged, by killing either the murderer or someone dear to them. If the murdered one's nearest relations failed to do this, they also would become vampires until honour was finally satisfied. This led to many endless vendettas.

In Scotland it was also widely believed until recently that if a cat or wild animal jumped over a corpse, the dead person would come back to haunt the living.

Under Eastern Orthodox Christian rules it was believed possible to judge the condition of a person's soul in the afterlife by that of their corpse, so it was once common

practice in Greece and Bulgaria to exhume corpses after
a year to see if their souls had gone to heaven, purgatory
or hell (plus of course to check they had not become
vampires). This still occasionally happens today.

A common folk remedy known throughout Eastern
Europe against turning into a vampire after having been
attacked by one was this: first track your vampire to its
grave and after beheading or impaling it, remove some
blood-soaked strips of its shroud and burn them to ashes.
Mix the ashes with some edible substance to make a paste
or broth and eat it. Alternatively, remove the heart and do
the same with that.

This remedy is far from forgotten. *The Scotsman* 31
January 2005 reported that in Romania six men from the
remote village of Marotinul de Sus were jailed for six
months for digging up the corpse of a 76-year-old cancer
victim and eating his heart because they believed he was
a vampire. They waited for seven weeks after the former
teacher died before exhuming his body and cutting out
the heart. This they cooked and mixed with ash and water
to make a soup which, they said, made them feel "much
better".

In their defence to the court in the southern Romanian
town of Craiova the six claimed that they had acted
in self-defence against "a well-known vampire" using a
traditional remedy. They were convicted for violating
a grave.

There was no glamour to the old vampires of Eastern Europe at the time when most people there believed unquestioningly in them. They did not seduce their victims, they simply attacked them or at most tried to lure them out into the night by calling their names. For which reason people often refused to answer calls at night, though in Greece they believe a vampire can only call out once, so if a voice calls out three times it is probably safe.

One hates to think about those unfortunates buried before they were quite dead – waking in the grave, struggling free and staggering home only to be greeted as vampires, which must have often happened in times of plague. Possibly they even believed themselves that they had become vampires.

The modern glamour of the vampire comes largely from the poetry and fiction of the past couple of centuries, which have blended the East European vampire with more ancient bloodsucking seductresses like the *lamia*.

The success of this can be seen in a survey by the Vampire Research Center in New York which revealed that 80% of female respondents claimed they would sleep with a vampire given the chance.

The Vampire Research Center was established in New York in 1972 by Dr Stephen Kaplan who twenty years later claimed to have over a thousand 'real' vampires on

his books; 'real' vampires being people claiming a physical or psychological need to drink blood, as opposed to 'vampiroids' who just like dressing the part.

These 'real' vampires claimed to get their blood from consenting partners, either through informal groupings or by joining clubs of like-minded people. In one notable club in New York donors lay on a bar with taps plugged into their veins ready for customers. Enthusiasts tend to be more careful, however, since the spread of AIDS.

In his 1993 book *The Monster Show* author David J Skal interviewed many such 'real vampires' and their blood donors. Apart from their taste for human blood many led otherwise perfectly normal lives and some were even otherwise vegetarian.

CHAPTER I

The Blood is the Life: Myths and Legends

I N ANCIENT GREECE AND ROME the vampire they feared was the bloodthirsty *lamia*. Originally this was the name of a goddess whose children were all killed by a jealous rival and who went mad as a result, taking out her revenge on humans. Later it became the term for a whole horde of bloodthirsty female demons that, jealous of human mothers, preyed on their men and babies. In the Middle Ages they became known as *succubae* and were often depicted as women who were snakes from the waist down. They could also take the form of owls.

In John Keats' 1819 poem *Lamia* she is a scary serpentine demon who persuades Hermes to transform her into a beautiful maid so she can seduce and marry a young man with whom she has fallen in love; but the sage Appollonius of Tyana breaks the spell at their wedding feast, to the groom's distress:

"Lamia!" he shriek'd; and nothing but the shriek
With its sad echo did the silence break.
"Begone, foul dream!" he cried, gazing again
In the bride's face, where now no azure vein
Wander'd on fair-spaced temples; no soft bloom
Misted the cheek; no passion to illume
The deep-recessed vision: - all was blight;
Lamia, no longer fair, there sat a deadly white.

Empusa in Greek legend was a demonic daughter of the witch goddess Hecate. While usually a monster with brazen feet, she could transform herself into a beautiful maiden to seduce men in their sleep and drain their life force. Her name also later became a general term for similar semen- and bloodsucking spirits.

In Arabic lore vampires are also usually, though not always, female and are very similar to *lamiae*, often using their physical charms to secure dinner. Also called *affrits* or simply ghouls, they are as interested in eating firm young flesh as in drinking blood. When fresh meat is not available they gather in cemeteries and feast on fresh corpses.

The ghoul will be familiar to readers of *The Arabian Nights* where, on the fifth night, Scheherezade tells the tale of the Prince and the Envious Vizier. In complete editions of the *Nights* a similar ghoulish enchantress features in the tale of Sidi Nouman.

THE TALE OF
SIDI NOUMAN

The *Thousand and One Nights* tells us that there
was once a wealthy young man called Sidi
Nouman who married a beautiful maiden called
Amina. As was the custom those days, he was not
allowed to see her before the wedding so was
greatly relieved to find that she was quite as beautiful and charming as he had been promised.
There was just one thing a bit odd about her
which he noticed at their first meal together. The
table was piled with delicacies but all she ate was
a few grains of rice, one by one with a long pin,
and a few crumbs of bread – scarcely enough to
feed a sparrow. The same happened at the meals
that followed despite Sidi Nouman's cajoling.

Then one night when she must have thought
him asleep, he heard her leave their bed so he quietly rose too and followed. Under a bright moon
he followed her out into the street and then
towards a cemetery, which she entered. Creeping
through the tombs, Sidi came across her chatting
in a very friendly way with a dreadful ghoul. They
proceeded to dig up a corpse that had been buried
that day, which they feasted upon merrily, chatting
all the while like old friends. Finally they threw the
remains of the body back into the grave and
reburied it with earth.

Sidi Nouman crept home and said nothing

when Amina returned to bed. Nor did he say anything all the next day but at dinner when she was picking at her rice as usual, finally his patience burst and he said: "Amina, you must have guessed my surprise when the day after our marriage you declined to eat anything but a few morsels. However I had patience and only tried to tempt your appetite by the choicest dishes I could invent, but all to no avail. Still, Amina, it seems to me that there must be some dish among them as sweet-tasting as the flesh of a corpse?"

Amina was furious at being discovered and, casting a quick spell over a jug of water, she dashed it in his face with the words: "Wretch, receive the reward of your prying, and become a dog." Which indeed he did and she chased him around the house with a stick trying to beat the life out of him.

Luckily he escaped and went wandering for a time in the form of a dog, scavenging as best he could while Amina continued in the luxury of his home, lamenting to all around the sudden disappearance of her husband. Finally Sidi Nouman happened to meet a maiden skilled in white magic who guessed what had happened and restored him to his true form. She also gave him a magic potion which he then splashed upon Amina with the words: "Receive the punishment of thy wickedness!" and transformed her into a mare, which was led off to the stables and made to work hard for its hay with frequent beatings.

Close to, or identical with, the *lamia* in Rome was the *stryx* or screech owl, which is related to the Indian term for a vampire *strigon* and the Romanian word *strigoi*. Originally in Romania this meant a witch who prowled the night in the form of an owl seeking human blood but by the nineteenth century it came to refer to the neglected dead who were unable to rest in their graves, as mentioned in a Baedeker travel guide that was one of Bram Stoker's chief sources for descriptions of Transylvania, which he never actually visited:

> *Strigoi are not malicious, but their appearance bodes no good and may be regarded as omens of sickness and misfortune . . . More decidedly evil, however, is the vampire, or nosferatu, in whom every Roumenian peasant believes as firmly as he does in heaven or hell. There are two sorts of vampires - living and dead. The living vampire is in general the illegitimate offspring of two illegitimate persons, but even a flawless pedigree will not ensure anyone against the intrusion of a vampire into his family vault, since every person killed by a nosferatu becomes likewise a vampire after death, and will continue to suck the blood of other innocent people till the spirit has been exorcised, either by opening the grave of the person suspected and driving a stake through the corpse, or firing a pistol shot into the coffin. In very obstinate cases it is further recommended to cut off the head and replace it in the coffin with the mouth filled with garlic, or to extract the heart and burn it, strewing the ashes over the grave.*
>
> *That such remedies are often resorted to, even in our enlightened days, is a well-attested fact, and*

there are probably few Roumenian villages where
such has not taken place within the memory of
the inhabitants.

Emily de Laszowska Gerard *The Land Beyond the*
Forest, 1885

In ancient Babylon such demons were known as *liliti*
while in Hebrew legend Lilith was Adam's first wife. She
was created from earth like him as his equal but they
argued over who should be on top during intercourse, so
she ran off to live with some fallen angels on the shores of
the Red Sea. When Adam complained to God he sent
three angels to fetch her back. They failed, but did destroy
all the offspring she'd had with the fallen angels and as a
result she swore vengeance on Adam and his descendants.
Some legends say that Lilith was the serpent in paradise
who tempted Eve to her destruction.

The Babylonians also believed in a monster called
Ekimmu, the restless spirit of someone who has not been
buried properly and so haunts the living, thirsting for
blood and life. As it says in the Epic of Gilgamesh:

> *The man whose corpse lieth in the desert -*
> *Thou and I have often seen such a one -*
> *His spirit resteth not in the earth.*

Jewish mothers in ancient times used to put amulets round the necks of baby boys bearing the names of the three angels (Senoy, Sansenoy, and Semangelof) who had battled Lilith, to ward her off. They also used to let baby boys' hair grow long so they would be mistaken for girls and left alone.

The ancient Hebrews were forbidden to drink animal (and so especially human) blood because it was believed to contain the soul. As Moses decreed in Leviticus (xvii : 14) "For the life of all flesh is the blood thereof: whosoever eateth it shall be cut off." Or in Deuteronomy (xii : 23) "Only be sure that thou eat not the blood: for the blood is the life."

Abraham's obedience in the Old Testament was tested by being asked to make a blood sacrifice of his son Isaac. The substitution of a ram at the last moment signalled God's disapproval of human sacrifice but suggests that the concept was not unfamiliar to Abraham.

In Book XI of Homer's *Odyssey* Odysseus summons the spirits of the dead from the underworld by offering them rams' blood, and hence a temporary renewal of life.

On his famous sea voyage Odysseus and his shipmates had to pass within hearing of the famous and deadly sirens, whose song no man could resist, even if it meant death. He cleverly blocked his crew's ears with beeswax and had himself strapped to the mast so he could hear

their deadly song without being able to act. Thus he brought about the sirens' demise because it was their fate to die the first time a ship passed by without responding to their songs.

These sirens had female faces and breasts but the wings and lower body of birds. They were in fact first cousins to the owlish *lamiae* and it was only later that the term siren came to apply to mermaids, who were credited with similarly fatal powers of song.

Because of the seemingly mystical, life-giving nature of blood it was in ancient times believed to convey a much wider range of blessings and benefits than those we now

recognise. Pliny recorded in his *Natural History* that the
Egyptian pharaohs used to bathe in human blood to cure
or stave off leprosy.

The Aztecs and other New World peoples believed that
offering the blood of young victims could ensure the
fertility of the land.

Constantine the Great was advised by Greek doctors to
bathe in freshly killed children's blood to cure his leprosy,
but compassion prevented him.

In ancient Rome human blood was believed the only
effective cure for dropsy, epilepsy and many other
ailments. The blood was taken from freshly executed
criminals and gladiators to treat the wealthy.

In the Christian communion service the wine is mysti-
cally transformed into the blood of redemption that
Christ shed on the cross, as the bread is transmuted into
his flesh. In the eighth century Charlemagne, after
forcibly converting the Saxons to Christianity then had to
ban ritual cannibalism, which is how they immediately
interpreted the communion service.

The great medieval Islamic physician and scientist
Avicenna (980-1037) recommended the blood of various
creatures, including humans, as medicine for many
illnesses.

The blood of virgins was considered especially potent and medieval virgins in Europe are recorded as willingly (or so one very much hopes) offering their blood to help heal others, especially wounded knights. This is reflected in Book 17 of Malory's *Morte d'Arthur* where Perceval's sister gives so much blood to heal someone that she dies.

Even in the eighteenth century the historian Gebhardi noted in *The History of Hungary* that: "The drinking of the blood of human beings is not a mark of barbarity even in our time, for epileptics are often allowed to drink from the still warm blood of newly executed wrongdoers." Countess Elisabeth Bathory probably knew of this remedy and, given the 'epileptic' fits of her childhood, it must have helped fuel her own blood mania (see Chapter III).

In India Kali used sometimes to be honoured with blood offerings to pre-empt her taking it by force. This Hindu goddess has many faces, most of them benevolent these days, but as Kali Ma she is a goddess of destruction who revels in the shedding and drinking of human blood. This is the aspect best known in the West thanks to Kali Ma's adoption by the murderous Thuggee cult that preyed for centuries on Indian travellers until their suppression by the British in 1830, an act that helped gain wide acceptance of British rule. The Thuggee's last leader Behram was personally responsible for about 1,000 deaths between 1790 and 1830.

In many cultures it is common practice to spill blood on the graves of the newly deceased to keep them at rest, or else mourners will lacerate themselves until blood flows to achieve a similar end.

Although throughout Eastern Europe the same general beliefs about vampires prevailed, there were regional variations. In Russia and Poland it was once widely believed that vampires walked abroad between noon and midnight.

In Greece vampire hunting was once a quite respectable profession on a par with being a healer or a scribe. Vampire hunters often claimed descent from vampires themselves as the source of their prowess.

One sign Greek vampire hunters look for is one or more small holes about the width of a finger around the grave. This is enough for the vampire to come and go as it pleases, leaving the main part of its body behind and travelling in a semi-substantial form that it can change as it wishes.

Another test for vampires is to get a virgin youth to ride naked through a graveyard on a pure black or white foal. The graves which the horse won't cross are those of vampires.

In many countries one way to foil a vampire is to scatter seeds in its path because for some obscure reason (like the

F ROM ARMENIA comes the tale of a vampire called Dakhanavar who lived in the mountains of Ulmish Altotem near Ararat, and who would let no strangers into the area to count its valleys. Anyone who tried was attacked in the night and had the blood sucked from the soles of their feet till they died.

Despite this, two bold adventurers came to try their luck and when night came they curled up together to sleep, each using the other's feet for a pillow. During the night the vampire came as usual and, feeling about in the dark, found a head. Running his cold hands down the body, eager to reach the feet, he found to his surprise another head.

"Strange," exclaimed the vampire aloud. "In all the three hundred and sixty-six valleys of these mountains I have sucked the blood of people without number, but never did I meet one with two heads and no feet!"

Saying which, Dakhanavar wandered off in bemusement and was never again encountered in that country. And ever since it has been known that there are three hundred and sixty-six valleys in the Ulmesh Altotem mountains, as many as there are days in the year.

vampire Count von Count in *Sesame Street*) it will not be able to resist stopping to count them.

In Belarus if you lay a trail of poppy seeds back to a vampire's grave it will be forced to return there.

══════ CHINESE VAMPIRES ══════

The Chinese have almost exactly the same idea of vampires as people in the West.

In China the vampire is known as a *Jiang shi* and is considered a demon that has taken possession of a human corpse, which it nourishes by feeding on other corpses or living humans. Alternatively, it is the person's own lower soul that revives the cadaver. This idea springs from the Chinese belief that each person has two souls - the *Hun*, or superior soul, which strives for heaven; and the *Po*, or inferior soul, which is inherently malign. Where the *Po* is strong enough, even the smallest portion of the body such as a toe or finger is enough for it to build up from into a vampire, particularly if exposed to the light of the moon.

Chinese vampires have red, staring eyes and claw-like fingernails. They are immensely strong and can fly through the air. Like western vampires they suffer from appalling halitosis which is often enough in itself to kill their victims.

THE WELCOMING MAID

A COURIER NAMED Chang Kuei was sent with an urgent Imperial message from Beijing to the provinces. Soon after passing through Liangxian he was overtaken by night and a furious storm. He was beginning to lose hope of finding shelter when finally he saw a light that led him to a humble cottage. He knocked on the door and was greeted by a beautiful maid who stabled his horse and welcomed him into her warmth and shelter. Not only that but she also invited him into her bed where, after all imaginable delights, she promised to wake him at dawn.

However, Chang woke late the next morning to find himself lying on a cold, hard tomb in a dense thicket, with his horse tethered to a nearby tree. Scrambling into the saddle, he rode on for all he was worth, but was still twelve hours late at his destination. When asked the reason he told the tale above. His superiors naturally thought it was just a colourful excuse, but a magistrate was ordered to look into it anyway. It turned out that Chang Kuei was not the only one to have met the Welcoming Maid in those woods. Further enquiries showed that a prostitute had once hanged herself there and lay buried in the very tomb upon which he had woken, and her description matched perfectly.

Those like Chang who had lived to tell the tale seemed none the worse for their encounter, but others had been less lucky. There were tales of strange disappearances, sudden deaths and brutal murders in the area. So the grave was opened and the body within was found to be perfectly preserved, plump and with a rosy complexion as though merely asleep. Under official eyes the body was cremated and from that time the haunting and murders ceased.

A good way of distracting vampires in China, as almost everywhere else, is to scatter grains of rice or other seeds in their path. Alternatively you can trap one by making a circle of rice around it.

The only sure way of destroying the *Jiang shi* is cremation, though often beheading and impaling one with a wooden stake will do the trick.

Chinese vampires are often described as being covered in long white or pale green hair, which is probably due to the commonness of grave mould in parts of China.

VAMPIRE COUSINS AROUND THE WORLD

There were no vampires in traditional Tibet because, the Tibetans used to say, of their practice of 'sky burial'. In this, bodies are dismembered and left on platforms for vultures to eat. Thus would-be vampires had no body left to reanimate.

Malaysia has two famous vampire cousins which under various names are shared by other countries of South East Asia. The first called *langsuir* is said to have originally been an extraordinarily beautiful woman whose child was still-born and had the appearance of an owl. Seeing this, the mother screeched with grief, clapped her hands and flew away in the form of an owl herself, with hideous claws with which she perches on the rooftop hooting in a sad and ominous way. Driven mad with grief, she preys on humans, particularly men and babies.

When not in owl form the *langsuir* appears as a terribly beautiful woman in an exquisite, perfumed robe of jade green. Her fingernails are as long and sharp as talons and often poisonous. Her shining, jet-black hair falls to her ankles and hides the hole in the back of her neck through which she drinks blood. She is extremely dangerous but it is supposed to be possible to tame her by cutting off her hair and nails and stuffing them into the unnatural hole in her neck. After this she might lead a contented and quiet life for many years and make a very good wife, but something usually breaks the spell in the end and she flies off again into the wild as an owl. In Indonesia she is known as a *pontianak*.

Malaysia's other bloodsucker is the *penanggalan* which has the appearance of a severed human head or torso with tangled hair, penetrating bloodshot eyes and a long protruding tongue. It flies on batwings through the night with its entrails dangling behind it. Like the *langsuir* it delights most in killing small children by sucking their blood, but will also feed on the blood of women in child-birth.

By day the *penanggalan* returns to the rest of its body and any witch with the power to become a *penanggalan* is sure to have a large vat of vinegar somewhere in her house, because the entrails swell up after leaving the body and must be soaked awhile in vinegar before squeezing back into it. Ways to guard against the *penanggalan* include hanging thistles and thorns around doors and windows, and spreading thorns wherever blood is spilt, because the creature is afraid of getting its intestines caught up in these.

One way to destroy a *penanggalan* is to find the body while the head is away and sprinkle garlic or salt into the cavity of its neck. This prevents the head's return and at daybreak it will die.

Mexican folklore has a host of bloodthirsty spirits, not least the witches known placatingly as The Ladies, or *Ciuateteo*, who like to gather at crossroads. They are said to be women who died in their first labour and are presided over by a Mexican Lilith called Tlazolteotl, goddess of sorcery, lust and evil whose totem creatures were the snake and screech owl.

The Ladies are very pale and fly through the air on broomsticks. They are liable to attack anyone they meet during the hours of darkness, but their special taste is for the blood of children. Any child visited by one of these vampires will soon waste away and die. To guard against this, rural Mexicans carefully seal their houses at night with charms and thorns, and leave offerings of tasty food at crossroads to keep the witches from wandering.

In India *rakshasas* are ghouls or demons that inhabit cemeteries, though given a chance they prefer eating children and pregnant women to corpses, which they can re-animate to prey upon the living. Half-animal and half-human in appearance, they have fangs and claws. They were first described in the *Arthava Veda*.

In Africa the Ashanti people of Ghana tell of the *asasabonsam* which is vaguely human in appearance but equipped with sharp iron fangs and clawed feet at the end of long thin legs. Their habit is to sit on branches over paths, dangling their legs like innocent vines till some luckless traveller passes below like a walking dinner.

The Ashanti also speak of the *obayifo*, a witch living unrecognised in the community who at night can leave her body as a ball of light and attack people. She is especially fond of the blood of children but will attack anyone at need. Under other names this kind of witch was feared throughout the Bantu tribes.

Among the Awemba of Zambia it is traditional to spill blood on the ground at mealtimes to honour and appease the spirits of the ancestors. They believe that spirits are able to draw nourishment from the blood. Also that evil people are able to rise from the grave to feed on the blood of the living, which means it is very dangerous to leave your own blood lying on the ground because a passing ghoul may get a taste for it and follow you home.

The best known indigenous Australian vampire is the *yaramayahoo*. This is a small red creature with tentacle hands and an enormous mouth. It is said to live in fig trees and drop down on passers-by, wrap itself around them and drink their blood. The victims usually survive but find themselves a little smaller than before. If attacked often enough they turn into *yaramayahoos* themselves.

PSYCHIC VAMPIRES

There are very real vampires commonly abroad in the world and known popularly in fiction and psychology as 'psychic vampires'. These are people who somehow manage to drain the energy out of their companions. The *femme fatale* is the most glamorous example reminiscent of the ancient Greek *lamia* – a devastatingly attractive woman who demands complete abject adoration from her suitors but inevitably breaks their hearts. In the 1930s such women were popularly called 'vamps'.

Arthur Conan Doyle's 1895 story about a psychic vampire *The Parasite* was published as a companion book to Bram Stoker's *The Watter's Mou*, and helped shape the character of Count Dracula, which he was working on at the time.

Franz Hartmann, a famous Victorian investigator of unusual phenomena articulated the idea of the 'psychic sponge' or mental vampire in an article on vampires in the magazine *Borderland*, July 1896, describing them as people who: "unconsciously vampirise every sensitive person with whom they come in contact, and they instinctively seek out such persons and invite them to stay at their houses. I know of an old lady, a vampire, who thus ruined the health of a lot of robust servant girls, whom she took into her service and made them sleep in her room. They were all in good health when they entered, but they soon began to sicken, they became emaciated and consumptive and had to leave the service".

In Iceland there is a strong tradition that a baby should not sleep in the same room as an old person because, however unconsciously, they may drain its life force.

Die facht sich an gar ein graussem

liche erschꝛockenliche hystorien von dem wilden reütrich.
Dracole wayde. Wie er die leüt gespißt hat. vnd gepraten.
vnd mit den haübtern yn einem kessel gesoten. vñ wie er die
leüt geschunden hat vñ zerhacken laſſen als ein kraut. Jtez
er hat auch den müterñ ire kind gepraté vnd ſy habés müſ
ſen selber eſſen. Vnd vil andere erschꝛockenliche ding die in
diſſem Tractat geschꝛiben ſtend. Vnd in welchem land er
geregiret hat.

CHAPTER II

Bloodlust: Vampires in History

VLAD THE IMPALER

*I have asked my friend Arminus, of Buda-Pesth
University, to make his record; and he must, indeed,
have been that Voivode Dracula who won his fame
against the Turk, over the great river on the very fron-
tier of Turkey. If it be so, then he was no common man;
for in that time and for centuries after he was spoken
of as the cleverest and most cunning as well as the
bravest of the sons of the "land beyond the forest".
That mighty brain and that iron resolution went
with him to the grave.*
Bram Stoker *Dracula* 1897

Before Bram Stoker there was never a hint in Romania
(which includes Transylvania) that their original Dracula
had become a vampire after death. He was in fact
remembered as a national (if extremely savage) hero, for
guarding the gates of Central Europe against the Turks in
the fifteenth century.

The historical Dracula, also famous as Vlad the Impaler, was born around 1430 in the ancient German fortress town of Schassburg. Now named Sighisoara in Romania, it lies some hundred kilometres south of Bistrita (where Bram Stoker's novel begins) and between the converging Transylvanian Alps and Carpathian Mountains. His birthplace survives as the house of a modestly rich merchant. Its only distinction from the rest in the street is a plaque declaring it to have been the home in 1431 of Vlad Dracul, Dracula's father.

Dracul in Romanian means both dragon and devil. It was a title bestowed on Dracula's father as an honour for his services to the Holy Roman Empire in its sense of 'dragon'. The word's double meaning was a linguistic coincidence that just happened to fit his devlish son very appropriately, though dragons in Romania were generally blamed for violent weather.

Vlad senior was Prince of Wallachia and Duke of Transylvania. As part of a truce with the Turks he handed his sons Vlad and Radu over to them as hostages for four years. They were kept in luxury but their lives often hung by a thread because of their father's devious political manoeuvring.

When Dracul was assassinated by his own nobles, the Turks released Vlad Dracula to take his place, hoping he would be a tame ruler. Fearing the same fate as his father, Dracula fled Wallachia and gradually built up his strength and support till he was able to seize the throne again by force, killing his usurper in 1456. Then he gave a clear signal of how he intended to rule (see overleaf).

The most famous of Dracula's massacres took place in the city of Brasov (now Kronstadt), when in the course of one grisly April day hundreds if not thousands of Saxon burghers were impaled at the foot of Tampa hill around the chapel of St Jacob. Because they had refused to pay trading taxes, Dracula stormed the city in 1459 which, besides the massacre, was looted and burned.

There were other massacres less famous but equally or more ferocious, such as that at Sibiu a year later in 1460. Then 10,000 of the mostly German citizens, men women and children, are said to have perished. Also at Fagaras and many smaller towns named in the German pamphlets, fore-runners of today's newspapers, which were the chief means of spreading Dracula's infamy abroad.

WHEN Vlad Dracula came to power in 1456 he summoned all the bishops and nobles, or boyars, to his palace at Targoviste. They came, curious and unsuspecting, confident that they were the real power in the land. They believed that Dracula, as with his many short-lived predecessors, could only rule with their blessing.

But Dracula had no intention of being their toy, and had neither forgiven nor forgotten his father's murder. He knew that many of his guests had helped or approved of it, and would dispose of him as lightly if the mood took them. So he asked each one how many Princes of Wallachia they had seen come and go. They were puzzled but replied openly enough, and even some of the younger ones could boast of having seen seven reigns.

Only those who could not possibly have had a hand in Vlad Dracul's assassination were spared.

A particularly nauseating custom Dracula cultivated was of feasting with his retinue in the midst of these forests, calmly enjoying the spectacle of his agonised victims as he dined. There's a tale of how when one guest complained about the stench, Dracula had him impaled on a stake high enough to raise him above it.

Not content with impaling his victims, Dracula also

The rest, some five hundred in all, were dragged from the palace by Dracula's troops and impaled live on wooden stakes prepared for the purpose. These stakes were deliberately blunted and oiled to prolong the agony as they slowly worked their way through the bodies of their luckless and squirming victims. Often it took days to die.

The survivors of this massacre were marched up into the mountains nearby and set to rebuilding Poenari Castle, which was Dracula's true stronghold (though Castle Bran elsewhere is often presented to tourists as 'Dracula's Castle') and from whose tower his wife is said to have leaped to her death. The unlucky noblemen worked at Poenari until their clothes fell off them, and then most often until they died. There were few survivors.

Never again did anyone with the misfortune to be questioned by Vlad the Impaler reply without thinking very hard indeed. He left in his trail neat forests of stakes topped by writhing or rotting bodies, applying his favoured form of justice on an ever grander scale to both Turk and Christian with equal enthusiasm.

devised many other ingenious tortures. He relished these openly and justified his actions with a paranoid logic that demanded nimble thinking from anyone who caught his attention.

There are two versions of how Dracula met his end. One tells how, his army having put the Turks to flight, Dracula climbed a hill to watch the slaughter. Being closer to the enemy line than his own, he disguised himself as a Turk and was attacked and killed by his own men, dragging five of them into the afterlife with him.

The other version says he was attacked during battle by traitors from his own ranks, which seems very probable. They may have dressed him up as a Turk afterwards to cover themselves.

In 1461 when envoys came from Sultan Mohammed II seeking diplomatic concessions, Dracula received them coolly in the throne room at Targoviste. When they bowed to him without removing their turbans, Dracula asked why they insulted him so.

"Lord," they replied, "this is our custom. We do not remove our turbans even in the presence of the Sultan."

"Very well," Dracula said, "then I would like to strengthen you in your custom." And he ordered that their headgear be nailed to their heads with iron tacks just long enough to do the job without killing them. Afterwards he said: "Now go and tell your master that he may be used to such insults from his servants but we are not. In future let him not try and impose his customs on the civilised rulers of other countries, but keep them in his own."

War followed.

Either way, Vlad the Impaler finally perished in 1476 at the age of forty-five. He is estimated to have personally ordered the death by torture of some 100,000 people, quite apart from the normal casualties of war, and his name inspired awe and terror in the hearts of millions more on both sides of the battle line.

Although Vlad the Impaler fulfilled all the conditions that Transylvanian folklore suggested likely to turn someone into a vampire after death, there was no hint of this until Bram Stoker wrote his novel. Possibly this is because the Turks beheaded him and took the head back to Istanbul as a trophy, while his body was interred on the island monastery at Snagov.

Vlad Dracula founded many monasteries besides Snagov in the hope that this would help him in the afterlife, though even when staying at Snagov he could not quite forgo his usual entertainments. He had a torture chamber built there and legend says that anyone praying by a certain statue of the virgin was liable to fall through a trapdoor onto a bed of sharpened stakes.

The claim to be the last legitimate bearer of the name Dracula is held by the German Prince Kretzulesco. He is not a blood descendant but was adopted by a claimant to being the last of the line, Princess Katharina Olympia Caradja Kretzulesco whom he befriended in the 1970s and who had no children of her own. At that time he was an antiques dealer called Ottomar Berbig. She formally adopted him after several years of trying in 1987, seven years before she died.

After taking the name Ottomar Rudolphe Vlad Dracula Prince Kretzulesco he became famous in Germany for taking part in a 1999 campaign to encourage people to give more blood to the German Red Cross. Shortly afterwards neo-Nazis tried several times to set fire to his castle at Schenkendorf in Brandenberg, south of Berlin, and he appealed through the media for an equivalent residence in England which he planned to turn into a Dracula attraction.

The castle has been the scene of several mass blood-lettings for the Red Cross and has a Dracula themed restaurant. The neo-Nazis apparently targeted it because of a prominent Jewish family that used to live there.

The Institute of Genealogy at the Romanian Academy denies any connection between the Kretzulesco and Dracula families.

ELISABETH BATHORY

Another real-life monster who has fed the vampire mythos is the Blood Countess Elisabeth (or Erzsebet) Bathory whose story has been retold in several films with varying degrees of realism. Notable among them are

Daughters of Darkness (1970), *Countess Dracula* (1971), *Blood Castle* (1972), *Ceremonia Sangrienta* (1972) and *La Noche de Walpurgis* (1972).

Elisabeth Bathory was distantly related to Vlad Dracula and born about a century later.

Bathory's atrocities were not on quite the same scale as the Impaler's but in some ways more blood-chilling. However tortuous his logic sometimes was, Dracula at least tried to find justifications for his tortures that put the blame on the victim. Bathory did not even try. She seems to have had little motivation beyond self-interest and sadism.

The Countess was born Erszebet Bathory in August 1560 in a part of Hungary bordering Transylvania, where her family originated. She was a member of one of the oldest and wealthiest clans in the region which contained cardinals, counts and princes, including King Steven of Poland who reigned from 1575-86. In her childhood Elisabeth suffered from occasional seizures that may have been epileptic fits, but she seems to have grown out of them.

Elisabeth was groomed for high office from the outset. She spoke several languages and was engaged at the age of eleven to Count Ferencz Nadasdy, the 'Black Hero of Hungary', whom she married at fifteen. They took up residence in Csejthe Castle in northern Hungary. With her husband mostly away fighting the Turks with the Hungarian army, in which he rose to become the most powerful general, Elisabeth had many affairs.

She also took to dabbling in black magic, guided by the professed witches Anna Darvula and Dorottya Szentes, and amused herself by inflicting harsh and ingenious punishments on her servants, having them beaten with sticks or horsewhipped for the slightest offence. One was smeared all over with honey and left naked out in the open for twenty-four hours at the mercy of insects.

In these tortures she was aided by her former nurse Iloona Jo and other accomplices, including her major domo Johannes Ujvary and a female servant Thorko.

Her husband occasionally disapproved of Elisabeth's excesses but more often fed her imagination with lurid tales of the tortures he and his friends practised on the battlefront.

Elisabeth was a famous beauty of her time and spent over half her day tending to her appearance. After her husband's death in 1604 she became ever more scared of ageing, despite still being considered a great beauty. Her torturing of young servants became ever more extreme, as if in some black magic way she was trying to steal their youth, or at least punishing them for having what she had lost. After her husband's death this got completely out of control and she began a ten year reign of almost unimaginable terror.

The legend goes that it all began one day when a maid snagged her hair while brushing it. Or some say Elisabeth merely spotted a fault with her headdress. Either way, the Countess was so furious she lashed out and blood spurted from the unfortunate girl's nose onto her mistress' face. When she wiped it off, it seemed to Elisabeth that where the blood had fallen her skin had become as clear and transparent as in youth.

Believing she had discovered the secret of prolonged, if not eternal youth, the Countess determined to bathe in the girl's blood. Summoning Ujvary and Thorko, she had them strip the servant, beat her and then drain all her blood into a vat in which she then bathed her entire body.

This soon became her regular habit in the early hours of most mornings. Over the next decade Elisabeth's accomplices provided her with hundreds more such victims, luring peasant girls to the castle with the promise of employment, after which they were thrown into the dungeons on the slightest excuse. Not content with stealing their lifeblood, the Countess devised ever more elaborate tortures for her victims, whose wretched lives were often prolonged for days and weeks as she first inflicted agony and then drained their blood. When Elisabeth grew tired from the exertion of her tortures, her trusted servants took over while she looked on, rewarding them for inventiveness.

All her victims were young females whom she often humiliated by parading them naked before the young men of the castle before being led to their excruciating deaths. On one famous occasion a group of them were soaked with water while out in the snow so that they froze solid.

Elisabeth Bathory's Iron Maiden, a human-shaped coffin lined with spikes, is said to have inspired Bram Stoker's short story *The Squaw* after he viewed it at Nuremberg, though actually the example there may not have been hers.

Another of her torture devices was a spike-lined cage beneath which she would shower in the blood of her victims.

Most of Elisabeth's tortures were carried out in the privacy of her dungeons at Castle Csejthe, but she also built torture chambers in other residences, including a mansion in Vienna where monks in the neighbouring monastery complained of screams that kept them awake at night and threw pots at the walls in protest.

The finding of bodies drained of their blood in the region around Csejthe led to rumours of vampires among the peasantry.

As she continued to age despite her atrocities, the Countess was persuaded by the witch Darvula that what she needed was the blood of noble-born virgins. So Elisabeth began recruiting as maids the daughters of lesser nobility, whose following disappearance was harder to explain than that of the peasant girls she had previously preyed upon. Several of their deaths were passed off with excuses, but suspicions were roused, rumours listened to and the net began to close in.

Finally King Mathias II of Hungary ordered an investigation that he entrusted to Count Gyorgy Thurzo, provincial governor and Elisabeth Bathory's cousin. On the night of 30 December 1610 he led a raid on Castle Csejthe and walked into a nightmare.

Entering the dungeons, he and his men first came upon the carelessly discarded body of a dead girl mutilated and burned beyond recognition and completely drained of blood. Further on they found two others in a similar state but still barely alive. Deeper in the dungeons they found more girls hanging naked in chains whose bodies had been pierced in many places and who had been used as living milch-cows for blood. They finally caught the Countess herself literally red-handed in the act of torturing another victim. Beneath the castle they found the remains of at least fifty other bodies for whom no other means of disposal had been found.

Countess Elisabeth Bathory refused to plead either way at her trial, and to minimise the damage to her family name she was never formally convicted or sentenced.

She was, however, walled into her bedchamber for life with only a small aperture through which food could be passed. She died four years later in 1614. Her accomplices were sentenced to horrible deaths, the witches being burned alive, and their confessions went on secret record which only surfaced years later.

Elisabeth Bathory's own records kept in her bedchamber put the number of her victims at 650, but the chances are there were many more that she found no time to note down. Her name was kept out of all official records for a hundred years.

VAMPIRE PLAGUES

In the eighteenth century there was an epidemic of apparent vampire activity in Eastern Europe and both court and military records have detailed accounts of hundreds of cases in which suspected vampires were found seemingly incorrupt in their graves and disposed of in the time-honoured methods of beheading, impalement and/or fire.

A related phenomenon that caused some heated controversy in the universities was that of the Chewing Dead or *Mastcatione Mortuorum* – corpses that apparently chewed their shrouds in the grave. This was the subject of a 1679 treatise by Philip Rohr called *Historical and Philosophical Dissertation on the Chewing Dead* which explained the apparent phenomenon in terms of demonic possession. This was refuted by Michael Ranft in his *Book of the Chewing Dead in Their Tombs* which claimed that the devil had no power to enter corpses. Neither they nor the many

other treatises that fuelled the arguments really explained
the matter in modern terms but the whole debate did lead
to the popularity of putting coins or stones into the
mouths of corpses to stop them chewing.

One of the earliest reported vampire epidemics was at
Khring on the Istrian peninsula in Croatia, where in 1672
Guire Grando is said to have risen from the grave to cause
many deaths and an epidemic of vampirism. In what was
to become commonplace in the following century they
found the corpse apparently incorrupt, bloated and with
blood in its mouth. Attempts to drive a stake through the
heart failed because it just bounced off and the vampire
gave a shriek which sounded horribly like laughter. So
they decapitated it, along with all of its apparent victims
and the plague seemed to pass.

Around 1730 an Austrian government report used the
word vampire (spelt *vanpir* in German) for the first time
in an official document regarding the case of Peter
Plogojowitz in Serbia, then under Austrian rule.

Plogojowitz was alleged to have risen from his grave in the
village of Kisilova in the Vojvodina region and caused the
deaths of up to ten people. The Austrian authorities called
for an official investigation.

The story was that in September 1728 Plogojowitz had
died suddenly at the age of 62. Three nights after burial
he had appeared at his home and asked his son for food,

which was given him and then he had left. Two nights later he had appeared again but this time the son refused him food. Plogojowitz left with a threatening manner and the next morning his son was found dead. Soon afterwards several other villagers fell ill with a mysterious wasting disease, complaining that Plogojowitz had visited them in their sleep and sucked blood from their throats. Nine of them then died.

When the army officers arrived they ordered all recent graves to be opened and found Plogojowitz lying as if in a trance, eyes wide open and skin flushed. His hair and nails had grown and there was fresh blood around his mouth. When a wooden stake was driven through his heart, blood gushed from every orifice to fill the coffin. His body was then cremated.

There being no obvious signs of vampirism on the other corpses, they were reburied but with garlic and whitethorn scattered in their coffins as a precaution. This appeared to put an end to the plague.

The other most famous case of vampirism on record from Serbia was that of Arnold Paole who was blamed for the deaths of dozens of people and cattle around the village of Meduegna (or Medvegia) near Belgrade.

Paole was a young soldier who had returned from fighting in Greece to settle on a comfortable farm in his home village. He was industrious, honest and seemingly healthy yet strangely reserved in manner. Eventually however he became engaged to marry Nina, the daughter of a neighbouring farmer. She loved him but felt there was some shadow between them. When she questioned him about it, Paole admitted to nursing a fear of dying young as a result of a misadventure he'd had while soldiering in Greece.

He had been stationed near Granitsa in a region where the dead were commonly said to plague the living, and had himself been attacked by one of these revenants. He had quickly tracked down and destroyed the vampire in the traditional manner but was afraid of having been infected in some way. This was in fact why he had left the army and returned home to early retirement.

He showed no symptoms of any illness however and life went on as before for a while, but then at the next harvest he fell from a hay wagon and died soon after from his injuries. A month or so after he was buried villagers reported seeing him around the village again at night. Several, who were named in the report, complained of being haunted by Paole, saying that after the encounters they felt weak and drained of energy. Then they began dying and as winter closed in panic gripped the village.

Three months after his burial the authorities arrived to disinter Paole's body. They found it seemingly untouched by decay and with fresh blood around the gaping mouth. After scattering garlic over the corpse they drove a wooden stake through its heart, at which it gave a piercing shriek and a great jet of crimson blood spurted out. Four of Paole's supposed victims were treated similarly (though there is no mention of their physical condition) and then all five were cremated.

The very detailed report on this incident was witnessed and verified by three army surgeons, a lieutenant-colonel and a sub-lieutenant. Written by Johann Fluckinger (or Johannes Flickinger), it was published in 1732 under the title *Visum et Repertum* (Seen and Discovered) and became an unlikely bestseller across Europe, leading to heated academic debate and widespread familiarity for the first time with both the name and characteristics of vampires.

> *Vampires issue forth from their graves in the night,*
> *attack people sleeping quietly in their beds, suck out*
> *all the blood from their bodies and destroy them.*
> *They beset men, women and children alike, sparing*
> *neither age nor sex. Those who are under the fatal*
> *malignity of their influence complain of suffocation*
> *and a total deficiency of spirits, after which they*
> *soon expire. Some who, when at the point of death,*
> *have been asked if they can tell what is causing*
> *their decease, reply that such and such persons,*
> *lately dead, have risen from the tomb to torment*
> *and torture them.*

John Heinrich Zopfius,
Dissertation on Serbian Vampires 1733

One cause of the East European epidemic is quite likely
to have been consumption or pulmonary tuberculosis,
which in parts of Europe and the United States in the
eighteenth and nineteenth centuries is estimated to have
caused one in four deaths. Typical symptoms of consumption are that the sufferer gradually loses strength and
appetite, turns pale and seems to waste away. There is also
breathing difficulty and, commonly, a dream of waking to
feel something sitting or pressing on the chest. All typical
symptoms attributed to the activity of vampires in fact.

Faced with a tide of rumours about vampires from
Eastern Europe the Church felt obliged to respond and
many scholars applied their intellects to the problem,
including Pope Benedict XIV. Most famous of them all
was Dom Augustin Calmet (1672 – 1757) a French
Benedictine monk renowned for his expositions of the
Bible.

Calmet's *Dissertations on the
Apparitions of Spirits and on
the Vampires and Revenants of
Hungary, Moravia etc.* a two
volume tome published in
Paris in 1746 was intended
to quash the spread of
superstition about vampires
but unwittingly spread them
even wider, thanks to his
faithful record of all the accounts
that came his way.

YPICAL of the stories which Dom Calmet preserved for posterity is this letter which he quoted at length: "It is your wish, my dear cousin, that I should give you exact details of what has been happening in Hungary with regard to certain apparitions, who so often molest and slay people in that part of the world. I am in a position to afford you this information, for I have been

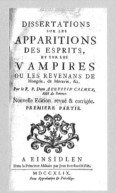

DISSERTATIONS
SUR LES
APPARITIONS
DES ESPRITS,
ET SUR LES
VAMPIRES
OU LES REVENANS DE
Hongrie, de Moravie, &c.

Par le R. P. Dom *AUGUSTIN CALMET*,
Abbé de Senones.

Nouvelle Édition revuë & corrigée.
PREMIERE PARTIE.

A EINSIDLEN
Dans la Princiere Abbaïe par Jean Everliard Kiliin.
MDCCXLIX.
Avec Approbation & Privilège.

living for some years in those very districts, and I am naturally of an enquiring disposition . . . This is the usual account, a person is attacked by a great languor and weariness, he loses all appetite, he visibly wastes and grows thin, and at the end of a week or ten days, maybe a fortnight, he dies without any other symptom save anaemia and emaciation.

"In Hungary they say that a Vampire has attacked him and sucked his blood. Many of those who fall ill in this way declare that a white spectre is following them and cleaves to them as close as a shadow. When we were in our Kalocsa-Bacs quarters in the County of Temesvar two officers of the regiment in which I was died of this languor, and several more were attacked and must have perished had not a Corporal of our regiment put a stop to these maladies by resorting to the remedial ceremonies which are practised by the local people. These are very unusual, and although they are considered an infallible cure I cannot remember ever to have seen these in any *Rituale*.

"They select a young lad who is a pure maiden,

that is to say, who, as they believe, has never performed the sexual act. He is set upon a young stallion who has not yet mounted his first mare, who has never stumbled, and who must be coal-black without a speck of white; the stud is ridden into the cemetery in and out among the graves and that grave over which the steed, in spite of the blows they deal him pretty handsomely, refuses to pass is where the Vampire lies. The tomb is opened and they find a sleek, fat corpse, as healthily-coloured as though the man were quietly and happily sleeping in calm repose. With one single blow of a sharp spade they cut off the head, whereupon there gush forth warm streams of blood in colour rich red, and filling the whole grave. It would assuredly be supposed that they had just decapitated a stalwart fine fellow of most sanguine habit and complexion. When this business is done, they refill the grave with earth and then the ravages of this disease immediately cease whilst those who are suffering from this *marasmus* gradually recover their strength, just as convalescents recuperating after a long illness who have wasted and withered.

"This is exactly what occurred in the case of our young officers who had sickened. As the Colonel of the regiment, the Captain and Lieutenant were all absent, I happened to be in command just then and I was heartily vexed to find that the Corporal had arranged the affair without my knowledge. I was within an ace of ordering him a severe military punishment, and these are common enough in the Imperial service. I would have given the world to have been present at the exhumation of the Vampire, but after all it is too late for that now."

Besides consumption, illnesses whose symptoms have been mistaken for vampirism include:

Porphyria: a group of hereditary illnesses causing extreme sensitivity to sunlight, sweating, racing pulse, stomach pains and vomiting, blistering and psychosis.

Human Rabies: usually caused by being bitten by an infected animal. Symptoms include loss of appetite, tiredness and insomnia leading to dementia, fear of light, water and mirrors and wild aggression. Death by rabies can leave blood in a liquid state longer than usual.

Anthrax: caused usually by inhaling field dust containing the bacillus. Symptoms include: tiredness, aching muscles, racing pulse, cough and low fever. It commonly affects people working with animals and can be fatal.

Photophobia: intolerance to light, which can be an effect of meningitis, migraine and certain eye disorders.

An epidemic of consumption or 'white death' hit New England in the late nineteenth century leading to a revival of belief in vampires. This led in turn to scores of bodies being dug up and mutilated to prevent them preying on their living relatives as vampires. The most famous case happened in Exeter, Rhode Island, to the corpse of Mercy Brown, often called the Last American Vampire.

It began in 1883 when local farmer George Brown was struck by the first of a series of family tragedies. First his

wife Mary, mother of their six children, took ill with
symptoms of consumption and over a few weeks slipped
into feeble helplessness and died in December. Then
the following spring their eldest daughter, Mary Olive,
began to sicken, complaining of terrible dreams and a
weight that crushed her chest in the night, making it
hard to breathe. She grew steadily weaker until in June
she also died.

For several years all then went well until around 1891 the
family's only son Edwin began showing signs of the same
illness. He was sent west to Colorado where the arid
climate was deemed better for his condition but in
January 1892 he heard that another sister Mercy had
died. This decided Edwin to return home as there had
been no noticeable improvement in his own health.

He arrived to find his poor father and some friends
convinced that the family was being preyed upon by a
vampire from within and it was determined to exhume
the bodies to see for themselves. Not all present that early
morning of 18 March 1892 were convinced. Certainly
not Dr Harold Metcalf, the district medical examiner. He
agreed to go along just to try and keep the situation under
control as an official witness.

At the cemetery Metcalf found that the bodies of the first
two females, Mary and Mary Olive, had already been
unearthed. He examined them and found their bodies

in a predictable state of decay. It being winter, Mercy's body had been kept in a crypt at the cemetery until the ground thawed enough for digging. She naturally looked much fresher than the others but to the doctor's eye after a quick autopsy there seemed nothing abnormal.

The others were less convinced. To them Mercy looked far too fresh in her coffin and also that she seemed to have turned on her side. Luckily they knew of a traditional remedy that might spare Edwin the others' sad fate. One of them opened up her heart with a knife and they were startled to see fresh-seeming blood running from it. So they removed the heart and cooked it to ashes on a nearby rock. Then they mixed the ashes with other ingredients to make a broth which Edwin was somehow persuaded to drink. It did little good though, because by May he too was buried in the cemetery. However, whether by chance or consequence he was the last of his family to die of the 'white death' and the operation was seen by many as at least a partial success in that the vampire had been laid to rest.

Despite her reputation as America's last vampire, Mercy Lena Brown is buried in the Chestnut Hill Cemetery in Exeter, Rhode Island, and her grave still attracts attention at Halloween, the gravestone being stolen by pranksters a few years ago. It was later found and returned to its place.

PREMATURE BURIAL

To be buried while alive is, beyond question, the most terrific of these extremes which has ever fallen to the lot of mere mortality. That it has frequently, very frequently, so fallen will scarcely be denied by those who think. The boundaries which divide Life from Death are at best shadowy and vague. Who shall say where the one ends, and where the other begins? We know that there are diseases in which occur total cessations of all the apparent functions of vitality, and yet in which these cessations are merely suspensions, properly so called. They are only temporary pauses in the incomprehensible mechanism. A certain period elapses, and some unseen mysterious principle again sets in motion the magic pinions and the wizard wheels. The silver cord was not for ever loosed, nor the golden bowl irreparably broken. But where, meantime, was the soul?

Edgar Allan Poe *The Premature Burial* 1850

Another likely cause for tales of the dead rising from their graves is premature burial. A hundred years ago in the United Stated it was estimated that there was one reported case a week of persons escaping premature burial. The number of those not escaping it is conjectural.

In the nineteenth century the fear of premature burial in Europe and the US led to a craze for grave alarms to warn of anyone reviving in the grave. Such warning devices could often be rented for a set period after death, then removed and re-used elsewhere.

MARTIN SHEETS was a successful business-man in Terra Haute, Indiana, in the early twentieth century. Being terrified of premature burial he devised a system for avoiding it. Rather than be buried, he had a mausoleum built so that his coffin could rest in the open. The coffin had catches that could be opened from the inside, and there was a telephone in the mausoleum so if he were to rise from his coffin, he could call for help from the cemetery office. Even if he was unable to speak, a warning light would alert them.

Sheets died in 1910 and although it was carefully maintained under the terms of Sheets' will, there was no sign of life from his telephone. Then, years later his wife died of a stroke while clutching a telephone so tightly, it's said that it had to be pried from her grasp. And when the mausoleum was opened for her to be laid to rest by her husband, the phone in there was dangling off its hook . . .

In Germany some mortuaries made it a practise to wait until there were visible signs of decay in a body before releasing it for burial.

Mystery writer Wilkie Collins (*The Moonstone*, *The Lady in White*) always carried a note like a donor card explaining the elaborate precautions his family should take in the event of his sudden death, to prevent the possibility of premature burial. Others in the nineteenth century spelled out in their wills the precautions they wanted, such as beheading or embalming.

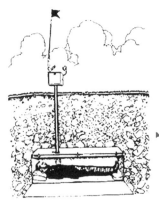

This ingenious device was invented in 1896 by Count Karnice-Karnicki, chamberlain to the Tsar of Russia. The apparatus consists of a tube connecting the coffin with an airtight box on the surface above. A glass sphere lay on the corpse's chest, connected via the tube to a mechanism in the box, so that the slightest movement of the chest would trigger the alarm. The box would fly open to admit air, a flag would be raised, a bell sounded and a light flashed to attract the attention of passers-by.

The annals of premature burial are full of anecdotes about people waking during the course of embalmment, usually too late and only very briefly, but to many this prospect was far preferable to waking up six feet underground.

In his book *Premature Burial* (1896) Dr Franz Hartmann collected details of more than 700 cases of premature burial, or narrow escapes from it. One example was of the famous French actress Mlle Rachel who in 1858 had collapsed near Cannes and been pronounced dead. She woke during the embalming process but died for real ten hours later from shock and the embalmer's wounds.

In the chancel to St Giles church in Cripplegate, London, before the church was largely destroyed by a bomb in the Second World War, was a memorial to one Constance Whitney showing 'her rising from her coffin. This was no reference to the Day of Judgement, it actually happened to her. She was buried while in a cataleptic trance and only woke when a sexton opened the coffin and tried to steal a ring from her finger.

REAL VAMPIRES

Nature has provided the animal world with countless parasitic creatures that live off others in a host of stomach-churning ways – leeches, brain-eating tapeworms, skin-crawling nematodes, mosquitoes, fleas, ticks etc.

Then there is the dreaded *candira* of the Amazon River, an excruciating bloodsucker from the catfish family. Take a pee too close to the river surface and it can leap up the stream of urine into your penis or vagina. Even if you realize what is happening and manage to catch hold of its tail, the chances are you'll be too late. It is also sometimes called the 'umbrella fish' for good reason, and the sharp spines point backwards . . .

Long considered a myth to frighten children and tourists, dramatic evidence for its reality was provided in 1997 when proof of the extraction of a *candira* (*Vandellia cirrhosa*) from an unfortunate young man's genitals was provided by urogenital surgeon Anoar Samad in Brazil. Not only could he produce a patient and a fish to back his claims, but also eye-wateringly graphic photos of the operation. The 23-year-old victim from Itacoatiara on the Amazon River had caught the *candira* by the tail just as described above but had been unable to extract it. It had then tunnelled through his urethra into his scrotum where fortunately it died, making extraction infinitely less messy than otherwise. After three days in its host it was five and a half inches long.

Many men are said to have cut off their own genitals rather than endure the *candira*'s burrowings.

In the absence of obliging human hosts, the *candira* burrows into the gill cavities of larger fish and feeds off the blood supply there.

However . . . not many of these bloodsucking parasites are actually graced with the name of vampire; perhaps because they usually only become nightmares after they have entered your life. A notable exception is the Vampire Bat which immediately caught the European imagination when tales of it filtered back from the newly conquered jungles of Central and South America.

Before this time bats had only been associated with vampires to the same extent as rats, spiders, snakes and the like, but suddenly all the night-fearing suspicions people had harboured about the little mammals seemed vindicated, especially in fiction where bats have become the vampire's necessary companion and favoured form for night flight.

The Common Vampire Bat feeds by cutting a small anaesthetized hole in its victim's skin and then lapping the blood that flows. It often gorges itself to the point of being unable to fly and then crawls off to a quiet corner to recover. Having a body the length of a thumb however, the blood loss to its victim is rarely enough to cause harm in itself, but the bat can transmit diseases like rabies.

Vampire bats do not particularly seek out human blood but will happily take it if the chance presents itself. An exposed human big toe is its menu of choice.

In the autumn of 2005 rabid vampire bats were blamed for 23 human deaths in two months in the northern Brazilian state of Maranhao according to the state health ministry, quoted by the Brazilian news agency *Estado*. About 300 other cases of being bitten by bats were recorded, but they were not fatal. Local experts feared an increase of the trend as vampire bats are driven from their natural habitat and attracted to livestock farms.

A prowler that humans don't have to fear because it lives about a thousand feet below the waves is the Vampire Squid (or *Vampyroteuthis infernalis* which translates as 'vampire squid from hell'). Its victims would probably agree with this name if they could, because it swims around in the lightless deep with long feelers adrift to feel out for prey which it then pounces on, but another reason it need not trouble our dreams is that it is only about a foot long.

In 1925 a specimen fished up in the Pacific between Panama and the Galapagos Islands by William Beebe's Arcturus expedition was described as a "small but very terrible octopus, black as night, with ivory white jaws and blood-red eyes". The eyes are, by proportion, the largest of any living creature.

When threatened, the Vampire Squid wraps its eight webbed and spike-edged arms up around its head to present a prickly, pineapple-like surface to the predator. Nevertheless it has been found in the stomachs of deep-diving fish, sea lions and whales. Sharing some qualities of true squid, octopus and jellyfish, the Vampire Squid is in a taxonomical class of its own. It was first described in detail in 1903 by German teuthologist Carl Chun.

The entire skin of the Vampire Squid is covered in light-emitting organs with which it can create spectacular light shows, possibly to confuse its enemies. It can also squirt out a fog of luminescence to cover its retreat

CHAPTER III

Shadows in the Night: Vampires in Fiction

THE FIRST REAL PROSE VAMPIRE STORY in English literature was the novella titled *The Vampyre* by John William Polidori published in 1819 and based on an idea by the poet Lord Byron, whose companion and doctor Polidori was for a while, supplying him with prescriptions for his drug habits (which he shared).

Because of Byron's involvement it was first of all assumed that he was the author and the book was enormously popular. The German poet Goethe called it Byron's finest piece of writing to date. When Byron disowned it, the story plummeted into obscurity, contributing to Polidori's death at the age of 26, probably from drug abuse or even suicide.

The Vampyre's outline was conceived on the same damp summer holiday at the Villa Diodati in Switzerland that inspired Mary Shelley's *Frankenstein*.

In mainland Europe the myth of Byron's authorship of *The Vampyre* was prolonged by publishers and its popularity inspired many copies and sequels by other writers in Germany and France. In Paris it led to a craze for vampire plays that were booked out for years. Especially successful was one by Charles Nodier which is said to have inspired a youthful Alexandre Dumas to write his own play *Le Vampire* with Auguste Maquet thirty years later in 1851.

Polidori's vampire, Lord Ruthven, established the aristocracy of vampires that has persisted in fiction ever since and was a direct inspiration for Bram Stoker's *Dracula*.

Although Byron disowned Polidori's tale, he took up the theme himself in this memorable curse from his poem *Giaor*:

> *But first on earth, as Vampyre sent,*
> *Thy corpse shall from its tomb be rent;*
> *Then ghastly haunt thy native place,*
> *And suck the blood of all thy race;*
> *There from thy daughter, sister, wife,*
> *At midnight drain the stream of life;*
> *Yet loathe the banquet which perforce*
> *Must feed thy livid, living corpse.*

The next landmark in English gothic fiction is *Varney the Vampire: or the Feast of Blood* by, probably, Thomas Preskett Prest, a prolific author of 'penny dreadfuls' who also brought to his public the evergreen tale of Sweeney Todd, the demon barber of Fleet Street whose business at no. 186 supplied the contents for Mrs Lovett's delicious

> *A*T LAST *[Father] Serapion's pick struck the coffin, which gave out the dull, sonorous sound which nothingness gives out when it is touched. He pulled off the cover, and I saw Clarimonda, pale as marble, her hands clasped, her white shroud forming but one line from her head to her feet. A little red drop of blood shone like a rose at the corner of her discoloured lips. Serapion at the sight of it became furious.*
>
> *"Ah! There you are, you demon, you shameless courtesan! You who drink blood and gold!" and he cast on the body and the coffin quantities of holy water, tracing with the sprinkler a cross upon the coffin. The holy dew no sooner touched poor Clarimonda than her lovely body fell into dust and became only a hideous mass of ashed and half-calcined bones.*
>
> Theophile Gautier *La Morte Amoreuse* 1836

meat pies, besides enriching him with whatever his unlucky customers happened to be carrying on them.

The legend of Sweeney Todd is believed to have sprung from an incident reported in the Annual Register of London in 1785 as follows: *"A most remarkable murder was perpetrated in the following manner by a journeyman barber that lived near Hyde Park Corner, who had been for a long time past jealous of his wife, but could in no way bring it home to her. A young gentleman by chance coming into his master's shop to be shaved and dressed, and being in much liquor, mentioned his having seen a fine girl home, from whom he had certain favours the night before, and at the same time describing her person. The barber concluding it to be his wife, in the height of his frenzy, cut the young gentleman's throat from ear to ear and absconded."*

This case is believed to have either precipitated or inspired the killing spree by the historical Sweeney Todd who was hanged in 1802 for a suspected 160 murders (though he was only tried for one that could definitely be proved) in one of the most sensational trials of the time. Prest used the known details as the basis for his penny-dreadful serial *The String of Pearls: A Romance* in 1846 which was quickly adapted into a stage melodrama by George Dibdin-Pitt that has been playing more or less ever since.

One of the star attractions of the stage show was a revolving barber's chair that flipped over when a customer's throat had been cut to reveal a new chair ready for the next customer. This was not a complete invention but a slight theatrical elaboration of the ingenious trapdoor device by which the original Todd despatched his clients to the cellar for butchering, disposing of the non-edible remains in the crypt of St Dunstan's Church next door, to which he had access by means of a tunnel.

> *There's a hole in the world*
> *Like a great black pit*
> *And the vermin of the world inhabit it*
> *And its morals aren't worth*
> *What a pig could spit*
> *And it goes by the name of London.*

From the musical *Sweeney Todd* by Stephen Sondheim

Varney the Vampire was first published in weekly magazine instalments and then as a complete volume of over 800 pages in 1847, the year of Bram Stoker's birth. Very few original copies survive because of their cheap paper but it has been intermittently reprinted and extracts have appeared in vampire anthologies ever since. The vampire is Sir Francis Varney, confirming the aristocratic trend in fiction for vampires.

The most famous female vampire in prose fiction is *Carmilla*, created by Irishman Sheridan le Fanu in 1872 on a much higher literary plane than *Varney* but with similar intent. It was filmed almost a century later in 1960 by Roger Vadim as *Et Mourir de Plaisir* (*Blood and Roses* in the dubbed English language version). The film updated the original story to the 1960s and starred his wife Annette Stroyberg in what is generally considered a classic, though more of lesbian eroticism than horror.

Hammer Films produced their own version in 1970 under the title of *The Vampire Lovers*, starring Kate O'Mara and Ingrid Pitt along with Peter Cushing and others who helped make it another minor movie classic. Ingrid Pitt also starred around the same time in the Hammer Horror classic *Countess Dracula*, Hammer's take on the bloody career of Countess Elisabeth Bathory of Hungary.

The original tale of *Carmilla* appeared in le Fanu's anthology of creepy stories titled *In A Glass Darkly*, the tales linked by the device of claiming them to be the case notes of one Dr Martin Hesselius. This was one of le Fanu's most successful books, published just a year before his death and still widely in print.

Carmilla was one of the main inspirations for fellow Dubliner Bram Stoker in making vampires the theme of his own magnum opus. For a while, apparently, Stoker even considered making his central character female, basing her on the bloodthirsty Elisabeth Bathory, but no doubt this felt too much like plagiarism. As a tribute to *Carmilla*, Stoker wrote a similar tale as a preamble to *Dracula*. This was dropped for publication but later published as an independent short story under the title *Dracula's Guest*.

When Bram Stoker's Dracula was published in 1897 many (though definitely not all) reviews in the London papers recognized the birth of a classic but the first print sold less than 3,000 copies and it did not really begin to sell well until after Stoker's death in 1912, since when it has remained continuously in print.

> *In seeking a parallel to this weird, powerful and*
> *horrible story, our minds revert to such tales as*
> *The Mysteries of Udolpho, Frankenstein,*
> *Wuthering Heights, The Fall of the House of Usher*
> *and Marjery of Quelher. But Dracula is*
> *even more appalling in its gloomy fascination*
> *than any one of these!*

London *Daily Mail*

Stoker was fond of claiming that *Dracula* was inspired by a nightmare following an over-indulgent dinner of dressed crab, but this was at best only partly true. He had already immersed himself in all the literature mentioned above and more.

Another significant inspiration was a travelling Professor of Oriental Languages from Budapest University, Arminius Vambery, whom Stoker entertained at the Beefsteak Rooms of the Lyceum Theatre in London, which he managed for Sir Henry Irving. This was an exclusive restaurant used for entertaining distinguished guests, including the Prince of Wales, Randolph Churchill and Sarah Bernhardt.

Vambery amused the company with fanciful tales of his adventures as a spy in the Middle East and also intrigued Stoker with tales about the infamous fifteenth century Romanian tyrant Vlad Dracula. There's dispute about how much he told Stoker and how much Stoker learned from his own researches, but whatever the truth Stoker was grateful enough to mention Vambery in the novel as an authority on Dracula.

Dracula's success in the theatre began in 1924 with an adaptation by Hamilton Deane, whose grandfather happened to have been the Stokers' neighbour in Dublin. Deane was manager of a touring theatrical company which played to packed houses around Britain, everywhere but London where with true metropolitan snobbery he was dismissed as a provincial ham. But given the immediate popularity of *Dracula*, in 1927 he boldly took his production to London where the critics poured acid on his presumption; but the audiences flocked in and the show ran to almost 400 performances, at which fainting in the aisles became a regular occurrence. Thereafter Dracula became a staple of Deane's repertoire for almost the rest of his life.

At Deane's London performances it became customary to station a nurse at the entrance to the theatre beside a notice warning those of a nervous disposition not to enter.

In the United States the play opened on Broadway in 1927 with the unknown Hungarian Bela Lugosi taking the title role, little realizing that he would never really escape the part. The United States and Canada were both taken by storm and the enthusiasm for stage vampires has continued more or less down to the present day, with only mild cyclical ups and downs.

In the cinema the first noteworthy vampire film was F.W. Murnau's famous, thinly disguised version of *Dracula* titled *Nosferatu*, filmed in Berlin in 1922 by Prana Films with the action transposed from England to Bremen in Germany, and starring Max Schreck as the startlingly grotesque vampire count. As Murnau had neglected to get permission he was successfully sued for breach of copyright by Florence Stoker and all copies of the film were ordered to be destroyed. Luckily at least one survived to become a silent classic that was successfully remade in 1979 by Werner Herzog and starring Klaus Kinsky and Isabelle Adjani.

After Murnau's false start, the real genesis of *Dracula* on the silver screen and hence worldwide fame was the Universal Pictures version of 1931, for the rights to which the studio paid Florence Stoker $40,000. Tod Browning directed the film, which starred Bela Lugosi in the role he made his own till Christopher Lee came along. In the uncertain climate of the Great Depression, the escapism of Browning's *Dracula* was an immediate and rampant success, particularly among women. Despite the villain's necessary demise at the end, it created an insatiable appetite for sequels that film-makers have been happy to feed ever since, reviving the Count in endless ingenious ways.

Curiously, given that vampirism has often been read as a metaphor for drug abuse (among many other vices), Lugosi claimed it was the pressures of filming *Dracula* that set him on the path of morphine addiction that was eventually to kill him. Lugosi died in 1956, the same year that Christopher Lee took on the role for Hammer Films in Britain.

One of Stoker's other novels *The Jewel of Seven Stars* is often credited with having inspired the whole genre of Egyptian mummy films. Published in 1903, the story tells of an embalmed Egyptian princess who returns to life with devastating consequences. It was inspired by a real mummy (supposedly of a princess) that Stoker had seen on holiday in Whitby some ten or fifteen years earlier. This was owned by George Elliot MP who had acquired it along with other antiquities during a spell of duty as advisor to the Ottoman viceroy of Egypt. When Stoker's scary book was published Elliot donated the mummy to Whitby Museum, who in turn passed it on to the museum in Hull where it remains, having survived a bombing in the Second World War.

Since *Dracula* was first published over a century ago countless other authors have tackled the theme of vampires with varying degrees of success. Probably many are much better plotted and written than Stoker's masterpiece but the only books which have impinged on the consciousness of the general reading public to anything like the same degree is Anne Rice's *Vampire Chronicles* series, begun with *Interview With the Vampire* in 1976. In this, like Stoker, she has been helped by the cinema and the masterly 1994 movie, with an all star cast headed by Brad Pitt and Tom Cruise, which brought her writing to the attention of audiences outside the genre.

LANDMARK VAMPIRE MOVIES

Over 800 vampire films are estimated to have been made since the birth of cinema. Here is just a fleeting and subjective review of some that stand out.

◆ 1922 *Nosferatu*
F.W. Murnau's famous, thinly disguised version of

Dracula filmed in Berlin in 1922 by Prana Films, starring Max Schreck as the startlingly grotesque vampire count. A silent classic.

◆ 1931 *Dracula*
Universal Films production directed by Tod Browning and starring Bela Lugosi in the title role following his success with it on Broadway. Florence Stoker received $40,000 for the rights, the first significant sum she received for *Dracula*.

◆ 1932 *Vampyr*
Directed by Carl Dreyer, this was not a great commercial success at the time and its Surrealist elements and lack of many familiar ingredients of Horror puzzle and disappoint many viewers; but some regard it as a classic.

◆ 1958 *Dracula* (*The Horror of Dracula* in the US)
The start of Hammer Films' great cycle of *Dracula* movies and other gothic tales, this film directed by Terence Fisher introduced Christopher Lee as Dracula in striking, glamorous contrast to Bela Lugosi who had dominated the role since the 1930s. Hammer's other *Dracula* films, mostly starring Lee are: *The Brides of Dracula* (1960), *Dracula - Prince of Darkness* (1966), *Dracula Has Risen from the Grave* (1968), *Taste the Blood of Dracula* (1970), *Scars of Dracula* (1971), *Dracula A.D 1972* (1972), *The Satanic Rites of Dracula/Count Dracula and His Vampire Bride* (1973) and *The Legend of the 7 Golden Vampires* (1974).

◆ 1960 *Blood and Roses* (*Et Mourir de Plaisir*
[And to Die of Pleasure] in France)
Directed by Roger Vadim and based on Sheridan le
Fanu's short story *Carmilla*, a dreamy tale with lesbian
overtones.

◆ 1967 *The Fearless Vampire Killers*
Directed by and starring Roman Polanski with
Sharon Tate, Ferdy Mayne and Jack McGowran, this
comedy spoof nevertheless manages some creepy
moments.

◆ 1970 *The Vampire Lovers*
Starring Kate O'Mara and Ingrid Pitt along with Peter
Cushing, this is the first of a trilogy of Hammer films
also retelling *Carmilla*. The others in the series were
Lust for a Vampire (1971), considered the weakest of
the three, and *Twins of Evil* (1972).

◆ 1970 *Countess Dracula*
Despite its title, this Hammer film has nothing directly
to do with Dracula, except insofar as its subject was
a distant relation of the original. Starring Ingrid Pitt,
it is a melodramatic but basically historical tale of the
life of the Blood Countess, Elisabeth Bathory.

◆ 1971 *The Red Lips*
Directed by Harry Kummel and starring Delphine
Seyrig as a modern Bathory.

◆ 1979 *Nosferatu*
Directed by Werner Herzog and starring Klaus Kinsky
and Isabelle Adjani, this was a successful remake of the
original 1922 film that Florence Stoker had banned,

with a similarly grotesque Count combined with Stoker's original story, all shaken up to form a new blend.

◆ 1983 *The Hunger*
Directed by Tony Scott and starring Catherine Deneuve, David Bowie and Susan Sarandon.

◆ 1987 *The Lost Boys*
Directed by Joel Schumaker and starring Kiefer Sutherland, Jami Gertz and others, this teen movie pastiche of Peter Pan failed to move many critics but pleased its target audience.

◆ 1988 *The Lair of the White Worm*
Typically outrageous Ken Russell film based on Bram Stoker's second most famous tale and starring Hugh Grant and Amanda Donohoe.

◆ 1992 *Bram Stoker's Dracula*
Directed by Francis Ford Coppola and starring Gary Oldman, Winona Ryder, Anthony Hopkins, Keanu Reeves, Sadie Frost and Richard E. Grant, with Tom Waits as Renfield. Despite an opening sequence about the non-vampiric Dracula that turns Mina Harker into a reincarnation of his original wife that has nothing at all to do with Stoker's book, this is nevertheless one of the most faithful screen adaptions in mood and atmosphere.

◆ 1994 *Interview With the Vampire*
Directed by Neil Jordan and based on the Anne Rice novel, this ground-breaking movie starred Brad Pitt, Tom Cruise, Kirsten Dunst, Antonio Banderas and Christian Slater. Initially Rice protested strongly about

the choice of Cruise for the vampire Lestat but reversed
her opinion completely after seeing his performance.

◆ 1994 *Nadja*
Produced by David Lynch, written and directed by
Michael Almereyda and starring Elina Löwensohn in the
title role with Peter Fonda as a bumbling Van Helsing
(and less bumbling Dracula). This stylish and mannered
movie (so artily shot that one's eyes water at times trying
to follow what's going on) follows the adventures of
Dracula's twin children conceived in a passing fit of
compassion some two centuries before the present day
in which it's set. Loosely paralleling Stoker's original
story, down to having a Renfield and a Lucy and a hasty
journey back to Transylvania for the climax, the film
nevertheless branches out in many original ways.

◆ 1996 *From Dusk Until Dawn*
Directed by Robert Rodriguez to a screenplay by
Quentin Tarantino. Among the stars are George
Clooney, Harvey Keitel and Tarantino who find them-
selves trying to survive the night in a Mexican truckstop
full of vampires.

◆ 2002 *Queen of the Damned*
Starring the late R&B star Aaliyah, this adaption of an
Anne Rice novel received mixed reviews but, possibly
helped by the star's sudden death in a plane crash soon
after filming it, has a cult following.

◆ 2002 *Dracula: Pages from a Virgin's Diary*
Filmed in mostly silent black and white, this Guy
Maddin film was adapted from a dance show and acted
by the Winnipeg Ballet's dancers.

CHAPTER IV

Just when you thought it was safe... Modern Vampires

ALTHOUGH FOR MOST OF US vampires long ago passed into the realms of pure fiction and metaphor, for some they remain a terrifying and blood-curdling reality; while for others, especially in North America, they have become a lifestyle choice in which no violence (or immortality for that matter) is involved.

The twentieth century produced many famous monsters who stunned the world by carrying their bloodthirsty fantasies through into reality. And even more whose exploits were just as bloody but who didn't catch the headlines.

In Germany there was the vampire/werewolf of Hanover, Fritz Haarman, who seduced young men before biting out their throats and then chopping them up to sell as black-market meat in the dark, desperate days of the 1920s.

VAMPIRE BRAIN.
PLAN TO PRESERVE IT FOR SCIENCE

Berlin. Thursday, 16 April 1925

The body of Fritz Haarmann, executed yesterday at Hanover for twenty seven murders, will not be buried until it has been examined at Gottingen University. Owing to the exceptional character of the crimes - most of Haarmann's victims were bitten to death - the case aroused tremendous interest among German scientists. It is probable that Haarmann's brain will be removed and preserved by the University authorities.

London *Daily Express*

There was also the Vampire of Dusseldorf, Peter Kurten, sentenced to death nine times over in 1931 for the sadistic murder of at least nine, but probably many more women and girls, in which he relished drinking their blood as they died. At his last meal before his beheading he speculated about whether he would be conscious enough to hear the blood gushing from his own neck, telling the prison psychiatrist: "That would be the pleasure to end all pleasures."

In England in the 1940s there surfaced John George Haigh whose custom was to drink a glass of his victims' blood before disposing of their bodies in an acid bath in Crawley, Sussex. He claimed his bloodlust had been triggered by a road crash during the war, in which he had been a fire-fighter in London during the Blitz. He was hanged in 1949.

Then there was the Forest Strip Vampire of Rostov in Russia, who between 1978 and 1990 killed at least 53 people, mostly schoolchildren, to drink their blood and cannibalise them.

The United States had its share of serial killers in the twentieth century, some of whom had vampire tendencies. One of them was Richard Trenton Chase who in his eventual confession claimed to have developed the conviction that he suffered from a poisoning that turned his blood to powder, and that he had to drink fresh blood to survive. He began by killing animals – rabbits, neighbourhood pets and the like – even buying dogs that he took home to torture and kill.

Then at the end of 1977 he went on a killing spree and gruesomely killed five people before he was caught, drinking their blood and mutilating the bodies savagely. He claimed that he needed the blood and had grown tired of hunting and killing animals.

The FBI still uses the Chase case as a model for the 'disorganised killer' and in 1992 a film called *Unspeakable* also used it as a template. Distributed by MGM, it starred Dennis Hopper and Dina Meyer and was directed by Thomas J Wright.

Another modern murderer from West Lothian, Scotland, claiming vampiric urges as mitigation of his crime, was Allan Menzies, who killed his lifelong best friend Thomas

McKendrick in a violent frenzy. Menzies had previously been gaoled for two years for knifing a bully at school and seemed moody and changed on his return, but McKendrick continued to hang around with him. After failing to get into the army or find any other employment, Menzies' moods deepened.

Then he became obsessed with the film *Queen of the Damned* whose star Aaliyah died in a plane crash shortly after filming. He later claimed in court that she regularly appeared to him in hallucinations, urging him to become a vampire in his next life by drinking human blood. Finally he had given in and killed his best friend. Menzies claimed to have drunk his blood and eaten some of his brains before hiding the body, and there were signs that at least the first was true. Despite his claims, Menzies was considered sane and convicted of murder. He committed suicide after two years in prison on 15 November 2004.

Not all vampires are violent and predatory though. In 1990 a similar conviction that he needed fresh human blood to survive seized 21-year-old Octavio Flores from Junin, Peru. The trouble was that he was afraid of catching AIDS so the only blood he dared drink was his own. After a few months of doing so he was hospitalised with acute anaemia.

Then in the wake of the film *Interview With the Vampire* in 1994, 27-year-old Los Angelino Jack Dean 'came out' as a vampire to the press and told how he had been perfectly normal until a motorbike crash in which he lost so much blood he technically died. He was, however, revived and after four months seemed on his way to a full recovery, apart from finding that he was now obsessed by blood, hated the sun, felt lethargic during the day and could only function properly at night.

To satisfy his obsession, Dean claimed, he spent the first two months sipping his own blood from a jar that the hospital had given him. When this ran out, his accommodating girlfriend allowed him, once a month or so, to make small cuts in her back and sip the welling blood. Dean said that drinking blood gave him a great rush of energy and a feeling of tremendous excitement but, contrary to some expectations, he was totally immune to crucifixes and still enjoyed large doses of garlic in his food.

In the 1990s the world's tabloids filled with news of a strange new bogey monster that seemed to sweep in an epidemic across Latin America. This was the *chupacabras* (or 'goatsucker' in Spanish) looking like a cross between a gargoyle and a kangaroo, with powerful hind legs and small, skinny arms. It stood four or five feet tall and was dark-skinned, with a spiked mane running down its back that sometimes looked like wings, red eyes, fangs and a ravening thirst for blood. Hence its name, though it seemed happy to drain the arteries of many other creatures besides goats – chicken, geese, cats, dogs, sheep and pigs.

The story began at Canovanas in Puerto Rico in 1992 when farmers began reporting the strange mutilation of goats and other farm animals. They had one or more deep

puncture marks in their necks and symptoms of serious blood loss. About thirty Canovans claimed to have seen a strange creature in the area leaping through the trees or prowling on the ground Their descriptions fitted what has come to be the standard description of a *chupacabras* but at the time it was like nothing they had ever seen or heard of before.

The loss of livestock continued and grew over the next few years, spreading out from Canovanas across the whole island and accompanied by reliable sightings of the strange creature. At the same time in Puerto Rico many strange lights were being reported, often associated with *chupacabras* activity and the rumour spread that the bloodsuckers (because it had become clear that there were more than one of the creatures) were either survivors of a UFO crash or the result of some bizarre interplanetary breeding experiment.

While alarming to the island authorities, the goatsucker panic escaped the attention of the wider world until late 1995 when Associated Press picked it up and spread the word. As the eyes of the world turned upon it, the creature did not disappoint, providing scores of character-istic and closely documented attacks that moved closer and closer to the Puerto Rican cities. In November the Canovanas paper *El Vocero* reported that the Goatsucker had attacked and chased two fishermen all the way home.

From Puerto Rico the creature seemed to spread across the Caribbean to Mexico where there was a sudden rash of both sightings and livestock drained of blood. From Mexico the *chupacabras* spread south as far as Argentina and north as far as Massachussets, fuelled by speculations in the Spanish language press.

No solid example of the *chupacabras* has yet been killed or captured and interest has waned, but occasional sightings and encounters continue to be reported today from all over the Americas.

In the Philippines the counterpart of the Malaysian *penanggalan* (bloodthirsty flying head and upper torso with dangling entrails) is the *manananggal* which is identical. In 1992 there was a curious outbreak of *manananggal* hysteria in the Philippines and for a while all the popular papers and TV newscasts were filled with accounts of sightings and even struggles with this vampire.

One witness, Martina Santa Rosa, described being attacked by a vampire with only the upper half of a naked body with wild, tangled hair, long arms and nails and sharp teeth. A neighbour backed up the story, saying she had seen the monster flying away from Santa Rosa's house.

An elderly woman suspect was even interviewed on nationwide TV by Cesar Soriano amid raging controversy over her claims of innocence of being a shape-shifting witch. The matter was resolved only when the reporter produced the dried tail of a stingray (a traditional test for witches) for her to touch under the beady eye of the camera and millions of viewers. When she managed it without flinching the suspicion passed elsewhere.

In October 2005 (as reported by the Indo-Asian News Service Raipur, October 17) Amit Soni, 28, killed Chhaganlal Sahu in order to drink his blood. Soni, a worshipper of Kali, had become increasingly worried about his mental health and thought the witchcraft ritual would help him. He told the police he had been practising witchcraft for some time.

Soni, a member of the local Home Guard, belonged to a poor family that lived in Mahasamund, 75 km from Chhattisgarh state capital Raipur. Witchcraft (and the fear of it) is flourishing among the tribal people of the area and is believed responsible for an increasing number of attacks against women, a phenomenon which led to the Witchcraft Atrocities (Prevention) Act in July 2005.

In Uganda and Kenya meanwhile, rumours spread around the turn of the Millennium that firemen were vampires, often aided by prostitutes who would trap their clients and hold them for collection by the firemen.

In Nairobi firemen arriving to put out a blaze would sometimes be greeted by children running away from them in terror.

In Malawi in 2002 CNN (courtesy of Associated Press) reported an outbreak of vampire hysteria that led villagers to beat one suspected vampire to death in the southern tea-growing district of Thyolo, and to beat and almost lynch three visiting Catholic priests that they also mistook for vampires. Though the government tried to calm fears, villagers took to sleeping with drums so they could call for help if attacked in the night.

So here in the twenty-first century vampires live on in many guises – terrifying, light-hearted and everything in between. In keeping with its shape-shifting reputation the vampire flits from one level of imagination to the next and then into reality, as we have seen above, with often devastating consequences. When we laugh at cartoon vampires we are laughing at our own fears and that may banish them for a while, but never completely. Drop any modern rational sceptic into a Transylvanian forest when the moon is bright and the wolves and weather restless, and he or she will soon taste the terrors that led the natives to evolve the strange beliefs that went into the shaping of Count Dracula and his successors.

Vampires tap into ancient fears and urges that have plagued us since the dawn of time. And there is no reason to suppose they will ever go completely away.

FURTHER READING

The Book of Werewolves
Baring-Gould, Sabine. Senate Books, London 1995.

In Search of Dracula
McNally and Florescu. New English Library, London 1973

The Man Who Wrote Dracula: A biography of Bram Stoker
Farson, Daniel. Michael Joseph, London 1975

The Un-Dead
Haining and Tremayne. Constable, London 1997

Vampires: Encounters With the Undead
Skal, David J. Black Dog. New York 2001

Vampires and Vampirism
Wright, Dudley. William Rider & Son. London 1914
Republished as *The Book of Vampires*, Causeway Books, 1973

Vampires Are
Kaplan, Stephen. ETC Publications, 1984

The Vampire in Legend, Fact and Art
Copper, Basil. Robert Hale, London 1973, 1990

The Vampire: His Kith and Kin
Summers, Montague. Kegan Paul, Trench, Trubner & Co.
London 1928
Reprinted as *The Vampire* Senate Books. London 1995
Abridged online edition: www.unicorngarden.com/vampires.htm

The Vampire in Europe
Summers, Montague. Kegan Paul, Trench, Trubner & Co.
London 1929
Reprinted by Bracken Books. London 1996